How the CRAYONS Saved the UNICORN

For Katie.
-M. S.

For Persephone and Athene.
-F. P. T.

How the CRAYONS Saved the UNICORN

written by
Monica Sweeney

illustrated by
Feronia Parker Thomas

SCHOLASTIC INC.

On the edge of a town, a lost little unicorn wandered in search of a friend.

He imagined all the fun he could have with someone
to play with, but in his search far and wide,
he couldn't find anybody to be his friend.

He splashed through a river, but the fish looked at him funny.

He looked up high in the trees, but the birds wouldn't sing with him.

He said hello to butterflies in the garden,
but they fluttered away.

So he kept on his search, *clop clop clop*...

...and made up games along the way.

"Roar!" he'd howl.

"Help me!" he'd cry.

"I'll save you!"
he'd chime back.

But after a while, he still felt gloomy.
Why wouldn't anyone be his friend?

Ever so slowly, his purple
hooves turned to gray.

His sparkly stars lost
their shimmer.

His rainbow mane and rainbow tail faded inch by inch,
lock by lock, until the rainbow was no more.

"Oh no!" bawled the unicorn. "Where did all my colors go? Where is all my sparkle?"

He sniffled, shuffled, shuddered, and sank.

In a soft tuft of grass was a little box of crayons.
All of a sudden, the box began to move,
and the unicorn perked up.

Out jumped seven special crayons!
Hey! who's that?!
Puh, puh!
Where are my clothes?!

The unicorn looked up brightly and said hello.
"I've been wandering for a while and I've lost
all my colors. Maybe you can help me."

What a great day! The new friends frolicked all over town,
clop clop clop, and spread their rainbow colors,
scribble scribble scribble.

The unicorn was as happy as can be.

He trotted through a field, and the crayons came with him.

He pranced in a garden, and the crayons pranced with him.

He hummed his favorite tune, and the crayons hummed, too.

They came across a great big puddle.

They hopped around the puddle and they splished and they splashed.

The unicorn looked down at his gray hooves in sadness. "What kind of unicorn am I if I don't even have my rainbow colors?"

The crayons surrounded the unicorn in a great big hug,
and the unicorn felt more confident and happier than ever before.

Ever so slowly, his gray hooves turned back to purple.
His sparkly stars started to shimmer.

His rainbow mane and rainbow tail came back inch by inch, lock by lock. But this time, the unicorn felt as happy as his very own rainbow.

ISBN 978-1-338-64366-4

12 11 10 9 8 7 6 5 4   20 21 22 23 24 25

Printed in the U.S.A.   40

First Scholastic printing, January 2020

Cover design and illustration by Feronia Parker-Thomas